MING LO MOVES THE MOUNTAIN

WRITTEN AND ILLUSTRATED BY
ARNOLD LOBEL

 A Mulberry Paperback Book   New York

Copyright© 1982 by Arnold Lobel
All rights reserved. No part of this book may
be reproduced or utilized in any form or by any
means, electronic or mechanical, including
photocopying, recording, or by information
storage and retrieval system, without permission
in writing from the Publisher, Greenwillow Books,
a division of William Morrow & Company, Inc.,
1350 Avenue of the Americas, New York, NY 10019.
Printed in the United States of America
First Mulberry Edition, 1993.
9 10 8

Library of Congress Cataloging-in-Publication Data
Lobel, Arnold.
Ming Lo Moves the Mountain / written and
illustrated by Arnold Lobel.
p.   cm.
Summary: A wise man tells Ming Lo how to
move the mountain away from his house.
ISBN 0-688-10995-0
[1. Mountains—Fiction.   2. Dwellings—Fiction.]   I. Title.
[PZ.L7795Mi 1993]   E—dc20   92-47364   CIP AC

for Crosby and George Bonsall

Ming Lo and his wife lived in a house at the bottom of a large mountain. They loved their house, but they did not love the mountain.

Rocks and stones broke loose from the cliffs. They dropped
down onto the house of Ming Lo. The roof was full of holes.
Clouds formed on the top of the mountain. Heavy rain fell
from the clouds onto this roof that was full of holes.
The rooms inside were damp and drippy.

When the sun did shine, it never warmed the house
of Ming Lo. The mountain always cast a dark shadow.
The flowers and vegetables in the garden grew
thin and sparse.

"This mountain brings us nothing but unhappiness," said the wife of Ming Lo. "Husband, you must move the mountain so that we may enjoy our house in peace."

"My dear wife," said Ming Lo, "how can one small man such as I move a large mountain such as this?"

"How should I know?" said his wife. "There is a wise man who lives in the village. Go and ask him."

Ming Lo hurried to the village. When he found the wise man, he said, "I want to move the mountain that is near my house."

The wise man thought for a long time. Wisps of smoke curled from his pipe.

Finally he said, "Go home, Ming Lo. Cut down the tallest, thickest tree you can find. Push this tree against the side of the mountain with all your strength. This is the way that you will move the mountain."

Ming Lo ran home. He cut down the tallest, thickest tree that he could find. Ming Lo and his wife held tightly to the tree. Running as fast as they could run, they pushed the tree against the side of the mountain.

The tree split in half. Ming Lo and his wife fell on their heads.
The mountain did not move an inch.

"Go back to the wise man," said the wife of Ming Lo.
"Ask him to think of another way to move
the mountain."

Again the wise man thought for a long time. Rings of smoke blew from his pipe.

Finally he said, "Go home, Ming Lo. Take the pots and pans from your kitchen. Hold a spoon in each one of your hands. With these spoons, hit the pots and pans as hard as you can. Raise your voice in loud shouts and cries. The mountain will be frightened by the noise. This is the way that you will move the mountain."

Ming Lo ran home. He took the pots and pans from his kitchen. Ming Lo and his wife held a spoon in each one of their four hands. They shouted and cried. They hit the pots and pans as hard as they could.

They made a great noise. Flocks of birds flew out of the trees, but the mountain did not move at all.

"Go back to the wise man," cried the wife of Ming Lo. "We *must* find a way to move the mountain!"

Ming Lo watched as the wise man thought for a very long time.
Clouds of smoke billowed from his pipe.

Finally he said, "Go home, Ming Lo. Bake many cakes and loaves
of bread. Bring these to the spirit who lives at the top of the
mountain. The spirit is always hungry. He will be happy to receive
your gifts. He will grant your every wish. This is the way that you will
move the mountain."

Ming Lo ran home. With his wife,
he baked platters of cakes and baskets of bread.
Together they began the steep climb to the top of the
mountain where the spirit lived.

They felt a strong wind as they struggled up the high cliffs.
It whistled and howled.

Soon the air was filled with flying cakes and loaves of bread.
There was nothing left for the spirit and the mountain did not move.

Without waiting for his wife to say a word, Ming Lo went quickly
back to the wise man.

"Help me to move this mountain so that I may enjoy my house in peace!" cried Ming Lo.

The wise man sat in deep thought for a long, long time. There was so much smoke coming from his pipe that he could hardly be seen.

Finally he said, "Go home, Ming Lo. Take your house apart, stick by stick. Gather all these sticks that are the pieces of your house. Collect all of the things that are your possessions. Bind everything into bundles with rope and twine. Carry these bundles in your arms and on the top of your head. Face the mountain and close your eyes.

"Having done all this," said the wise man, "you will step to the dance of the moving mountain. You will put your left foot in a place that is in back of your right foot. Then you will put your right foot in a place that is in back of your left foot. You must do this again and again for many hours. When you open your eyes, you will see that the mountain has moved far away."

"This is a strange dance," said Ming Lo, "but if it makes the mountain move, I will do it at once."

Ming Lo ran home. He took his house apart, stick by stick. He gathered all of the sticks and collected all of the things that were his possessions.

Ming Lo and his wife bound everything into bundles with rope and twine. They carried the bundles in their arms and on the tops of their heads.

Then Ming Lo showed his wife how to do the dance of the moving mountain. They faced the mountain and closed their eyes. Carefully, they began to move their feet to the steps of the dance.

They each put their left foot in a place that was behind their right foot. Then they each put their right foot in a place that was behind their left foot.

The neighbors saw Ming Lo and his wife walking backward across the fields with all of their possessions.

It was an odd sight and they watched in wonder.

After many hours had passed, Ming Lo and his wife opened their eyes.

"Look," cried Ming Lo, "our dance has done its work! The mountain has moved far away!"

Stick by stick, they rebuilt their house. They unpacked all of their possessions and made themselves at home.

Ming Lo and his wife lived the rest of their lives under an open sky and a warm sun. When rain fell, it came down gently on a roof that had no holes.

They often looked at the mountain that was small in the distance. There was happiness in their hearts for they both knew that they had made the mountain move.